The Celebrated Jumping Frog
of Calaveras County & Other Stories

The Celebrated Jumping Frog of Calaveras County & Other Stories
Mark Twain

PAPER + INK

The Celebrated Jumping Frog of Calaveras County & Other Stories
by Mark Twain

This edition has been published in 2018
in the United Kingdom by Paper + Ink.

**PAPER
+ INK**

www.paperand.ink
Twitter: @paper_andink
Instagram: paper_and.ink

The stories featured in this edition first appeared in
Humorous Masterpieces from American Literature ("The Celebrated
Jumping Frog of Calaveras County"), published in 1886
by G. P. Putnam's Sons (New York & London);
The £1,000,000 Bank-Note and Other New Stories
("The Million-Pound Banknote"), published in 1893 by
Chatto & Windus (London); and *The Man That Corrupted
Hadleyburg and Other Stories and Sketches* ("Luck"), published
in 1900 by Harper Brothers (London). Minor changes to
punctuation, spelling and formatting have been made.

1 2 3 4 5 6 7 8 9 10

ISBN 9781911475231

A CIP catalogue record for this book is available from the British Library.
Jacket design by James Nunn: www.jamesnunn.co.uk | @Gnunkse
Printed and bound in Poland by Opolgraf: www.opolgraf.com

CONTENTS

The Celebrated Jumping Frog of Calaveras County
7

The Million-Pound Banknote
23

Luck
69

THE CELEBRATED JUMPING FROG OF CALAVERAS COUNTY

In compliance with the request of a friend of mine, who wrote me from the East, I called on good-natured, garrulous old Simon Wheeler, and enquired after my friend's friend, Leonidas W. Smiley, as requested to do, and I hereunto append the result. I have a lurking suspicion that Leonidas W. Smiley is a myth; that my friend never knew such a personage; and that he only conjectured that, if I asked old Wheeler about him, it would remind him of his infamous Jim Smiley, and he would go to work and bore me nearly to death with some infernal reminiscence of him as long and tedious as it should be useless for me. If that was the design, it certainly succeeded.

I found Simon Wheeler dozing comfortably by the barroom stove of the old, dilapidated tavern in the ancient mining camp of Angel's, and I noticed that he was fat and bald-headed, and had an expression of winning gentleness and simplicity upon his tranquil countenance. He roused up and gave me good-day. I told him a friend of mine had commissioned me to make some enquiries about a cherished companion of his boyhood named Leonidas W. Smiley – Rev. Leonidas W. Smiley – a young minister of the Gospel, who he had heard was at one time a resident of Angel's Camp. I added that, if Mr Wheeler could tell me anything about this Rev. Leonidas W. Smiley, I would feel under many obligations to him.

Simon Wheeler backed me into a corner and blockaded me there with his chair, and then sat me down and reeled off the monotonous narrative that follows this paragraph. He never smiled, he never frowned, he never changed his voice from the gentle-flowing key to which he tuned the initial sentence, he never betrayed the slightest suspicion of enthusiasm; but all through the interminable narrative there ran a vein of impressive earnestness and sincerity, which showed me plainly that, so far from his imagining that there was anything ridiculous or funny about his story, he regarded it as a really important matter, and admired its two heroes as men of transcendent genius in finesse. To me, the spectacle of a man drifting serenely along through such a queer yarn without ever smiling was exquisitely absurd. As I said before, I asked him to tell me what he knew of Rev. Leonidas W. Smiley, and he replied as follows. I let him go on in his own way, and never interrupted him once:

"There was a feller here once by the name of Jim Smiley, in the winter of '49 - or may be it was the spring of '50 - I don't recollect exactly, somehow, though what makes me think it was one or the other is because I remember the big flume wasn't finished when he first came to the camp. But anyway, he was the curiosest man, about always betting on anything that turned up you ever see, if he could get anybody to bet on the other side; and if he couldn't, he'd change sides. Any way that suited the other man would suit him - any way just so's he got a bet, he was satisfied. But still he was lucky, uncommon lucky; he most always come out winner. He was always ready and laying for a chance; there couldn't be no solit'ry thing mentioned but that feller'd offer to bet on it, and take any side you please, as I was just telling you.

"If there was a horse-race, you'd find him flush, or you'd find him busted at the end of it; if there was a dogfight, he'd bet on it; if there was a catfight, he'd bet on it; if there was a chicken-fight, he'd bet on it. Why, if there was two birds sitting on a fence, he would bet you which one would fly first; or if there was a camp meeting, he would be there reg'lar, to bet on Parson Walker, which he judged to be the best exhorter about here, and so he was, too, and a good man. If he even seen a straddle-bug start to go anywheres, he would bet you how long it would take him to get wherever he was going to, and if you took him up, he would foller that straddle-bug to Mexico but what he would find out where he was bound for and how long he was on the road. Lots of the boys here has seen that Smiley, and can tell you about him. Why, it never made no difference to him - he would bet on anything - the dangdest feller. Parson Walker's wife laid very sick once, for a good while, and it seemed as if they warn't going to save her; but one morning he come in, and Smiley asked how she was, and he said she was considerable better - thank the Lord for his inf'nit mercy - and coming on so smart that, with the blessing of Prov'dence, she'd get well yet; and Smiley, before he thought, says: 'Well, I'll risk two-and-a-half that she don't, anyway.'

"This-yer Smiley had a mare - the boys called her the 'fifteen-minute nag', but that was only in fun, you know, because, of course, she was faster than that - and he used to win money on that horse, for all she was so slow and always had the asthma, or the distemper, or the consumption, or something of that kind. They used to give her two or three hundred yards' start, and then pass her under way; but always at the fag-end of the race, she'd get excited and desperate-like, and come cavorting and straddling up, and scattering her legs around limber, sometimes in the air, and sometimes out to one side amongst the fences, and kicking up *more* dust, and raising *more* racket with her coughing and sneezing and blowing her nose - and always fetch up at the stand just about a neck ahead, as near as you could cipher it down.

"And he had a little small bull pup, that to look at him you'd think he wan't worth a cent, but to set around and look ornery, and lay for a chance to steal something. But as soon as the money was up on him, he was a different dog; his under-jaw'd begin to stick out like the fo'castle of a steamboat, and his teeth would uncover and shine savage like the furnaces. And a dog might tackle him, and bully-rag him, and bite him, and throw him over his shoulder two or three times, and Andrew Jackson - which was the name of the pup - Andrew Jackson would never let on but what he was satisfied, and hadn't expected nothing else, and the bets being doubled and doubled on the other side all the time, till the money was all up; and then all of a sudden he would grab that other dog jest by the j'int of his hind leg and freeze to it - not chaw, you understand, but only jest grip and hang on till they threwed up the sponge, if it was a year. Smiley always come out winner on that pup, till he harnessed a dog once that didn't have no hind legs, because they'd been sawed off by a circular saw, and when the thing had gone along far enough, and the money was all up, and he come to make a snatch for his pet holt, he saw in a minute how he'd been imposed on, and how the other dog had him in the door, so to speak, and he 'peared surprised, and then he looked sorter discouraged-like, and didn't try no more to win the fight, and so he got shucked out bad. He give Smiley a look, as much as to say his heart was broke, and it was his fault, for putting up a dog that hadn't no hind legs for him to take holt of, which was his main dependence in a fight, and then he limped off a piece and laid down and died. It was a good pup, was that Andrew Jackson, and would have made a name for hisself if he'd lived, for the stuff was in him, and he had genius - I know it, because he hadn't had no opportunities to speak of, and it don't stand to reason that a dog could make such a fight as he could under them circumstances, if he hadn't no talent. It always makes me feel sorry when I think of that last fight of his'n, and the way it turned out.

"Well, this-yer Smiley had rat-tarriers, and chicken cocks, and tomcats, and all them kind of things, till you couldn't rest, and you couldn't fetch nothing for him to bet on but he'd match you. He ketched a frog one day, and took him home, and said he cal'clated to edercate him; and so he never done nothing for three months but set in his back yard and learn that frog to jump. And you bet you he did learn him, too. He'd give him a little punch behind, and the next minute you'd see that frog whirling in the air like a doughnut - see him turn one summerset, or may be a couple, if he got a good start, and come down flat-footed and all right, like a cat. He got him up so in the matter of catching flies, and kept him in practice so constant, that he'd nail a fly every time as far as he could see him. Smiley said all a frog wanted was education, and he could do most anything – and I believe him. Why, I've seen him set Dan'l Webster down here on this floor – Dan'l Webster was the name of the frog – and sing out, 'Flies, Dan'l, flies!' and quicker'n you could wink, he'd spring straight up, and snake a fly off'n the counter there, and flop down on the floor again as solid as a gob of mud, and fall to scratching the side of his head with his hind foot as indifferent as if he hadn't no idea he'd been doin' any more'n any frog might do. You never see a frog so modest and straight-for'ard as he was, for all he was so gifted. And when it come to fair and square jumping on a dead level, he could get over more ground at one straddle than any animal of his breed you ever see. Jumping on a dead level was his strong suit, you understand; and when it come to that, Smiley would ante up money on him as long as he had a red. Smiley was monstrous proud of his frog, and well he might be, for fellers that had travelled and been everywheres, all said he laid over any frog that ever they see.

"Well, Smiley kept the beast in a little lattice box, and he used to fetch him down town sometimes and lay for a bet. One day a feller - a stranger in the camp, he was - come across him with his box, and says: 'What might it be that you've got in the box?'

"And Smiley says, sorter indifferent-like: 'It might be a parrot, or it might be a canary, may be, but it ain't - it's only just a frog.'

"And the feller took it, and looked at it careful, and turned it round this way and that, and says: 'H'm - so 'tis. Well, what's he good for?'

"'Well,' Smiley says, easy and careless, 'he's good enough for one thing, I should judge - he can out-jump ary frog in Calaveras county.'

"The feller took the box again, and took another long, particular look, and give it back to Smiley, and says, very deliberate, 'Well, I don't see no p'ints about that frog that's any better'n any other frog.'

"'May be you don't,' Smiley says. 'May be you understand frogs, and may be you don't understand 'em; may be you've had experience, and may be you ain't, only a amature, as it were. Anyways, I've got my opinion, and I'll risk forty dollars that he can out-jump any frog in Calaveras county.'

"And the feller studied a minute, and then says, kinder sad like: 'Well, I'm only a stranger here, and I ain't got no frog; but if I had a frog, I'd bet you.'

"And then Smiley says: 'That's all right – that's all right, if you'll hold my box a minute, I'll go and get you a frog.' And so the feller took the box, and put up his forty dollars along with Smiley's, and set down to wait.

"So he set there a good while thinking and thinking to hisself, and then he got the frog out and prised his mouth open and took a teaspoon and filled him full of quail shot – filled him pretty near up to his chin – and set him on the floor. Smiley, he went to the swamp and slopped around in the mud for a long time, and finally he ketched a frog, and fetched him in, and give him to this feller, and says: 'Now, if you're ready, set him alongside of Dan'l, with his forepaws just even with Dan'l, and I'll give the word.' Then he says 'One ... two ... three ... jump!' and him and the feller touched up the frogs from behind, and the new frog hopped off, but Dan'l give a heave, and hysted up his shoulders - so - like a Frenchman, but it wan't no use. He couldn't budge; he was planted as solid as an anvil, and he couldn't no more stir than if he was anchored out. Smiley was a good deal surprised, and he was disgusted, too, but he didn't have no idea what the matter was, of course.

"The feller took the money and started away; and when he was going out at the door, he sorter jerked his thumb over his shoulders - this way - at Dan'l, and says again, very deliberate: 'Well, I don't see no p'ints about that frog that's any better'n any other frog.'

"Smiley, he stood scratching his head and looking down at Dan'l a long time, and at last he says: 'I do wonder what in the nation that frog throw'd off for - I wonder if there ain't some thing the matter with him: he 'pears to look mighty baggy, somehow.' And he ketched Dan'l by the nap of the neck, and lifted him up and says: 'Why, blame my cats, if he don't weigh five pound!' and turned him upside down, and he belched out a double-handful of shot. And then he see how it was, and he was the maddest man - he set the frog down and took out after that feller, but he never ketched him. And -"

(Here Simon Wheeler heard his name called from the front yard, and got up to see what was wanted.) And turning to me as he moved away, he said: "Just set where you are, stranger, and rest easy - I an't going to be gone a second."

But, by your leave, I did not think that a continuation of the history of the enterprising vagabond Jim Smiley would be likely to afford me much information concerning the Rev. Leonidas W. Smiley, and so I started away.

At the door, I met the sociable Wheeler returning, and he buttonholed me and then recommenced: "Well, this-yer Smiley had a yaller one-eyed cow that didn't have no tail, only just a short stump like a bananner, and -"

"Oh, hang Smiley and his afflicted cow!" I muttered good-naturedly, and, bidding the old gentleman good-day, I departed.

THE MILLION-POUND BANKNOTE

When I was twenty-seven years old, I was a mining-broker's clerk in San Francisco, and an expert in all the details of stock traffic. I was alone in the world, and had nothing to depend upon but my wits and a clean reputation; but these were setting my feet on the road to eventual fortune, and I was content with the prospect.

My time was my own after the afternoon board, Saturdays, and I was accustomed to put it in on a little sailboat on the bay. One day I ventured too far, and was carried out to sea. Just at nightfall, when hope was about gone, I was picked up by a small brig which was bound for London. It was a long and stormy voyage, and they made me work my passage without pay, as a common sailor. When I stepped ashore in London, my clothes were ragged and shabby, and I had only a dollar in my pocket. This money fed and sheltered me twenty-four hours. During the next twenty-four, I went without food and shelter.

About ten o'clock on the following morning, seedy and hungry, I was dragging myself along Portland Place when a child that was passing, towed by a nursemaid, tossed a luscious, big pear - minus one bite - into the gutter. I stopped, of course, and fastened my desiring eye on that muddy treasure. My mouth watered for it, my stomach craved it, my whole being begged for it. But every time I made a move to get it some passing eye detected my purpose, and of course I straightened up then, and looked indifferent, and pretended that I hadn't been thinking about the pear at all. This same thing kept happening and happening, and I couldn't get the pear. I was just getting desperate enough to brave all the shame, and to seize it, when a window behind me was raised, and a gentleman spoke out of it, saying:

"Step in here, please."

I was admitted by a gorgeous flunkey, and shown into a sumptuous room where a couple of elderly gentlemen were sitting. They sent away the servant and made me sit down. They had just finished their breakfast, and the sight of the remains of it almost overpowered me. I could hardly keep my wits together in the presence of that food, but as I was not asked to sample it, I had to bear my trouble as best I could.

Now, something had been happening there a couple of days before, which I did not know anything about until a good many days afterwards, but I will tell you about it now. Those two old brothers had been having a pretty hot argument, and had ended by agreeing to decide it by a bet, which is the English way of settling everything.

You will remember that the Bank of England once issued two notes of a million pounds each, to be used for a special purpose connected with some public transaction with a foreign country.

For some reason or other, only one of these had been used and cancelled; the other still lay in the vaults of the Bank. Well, the brothers, chatting along, got to wondering what might be the fate of a perfectly honest and intelligent stranger who should be turned adrift in London without a friend, and with no money but that million-pound banknote, and no way to account for his being in possession of it. Brother A said he would starve to death; Brother B said he wouldn't. Brother A said he couldn't offer it at a bank or anywhere else, because he would be arrested on the spot. So they went on disputing till Brother B said he would bet twenty thousand pounds that the man would live thirty days, anyway, on that million, and keep out of jail, too. Brother A took him up. Brother B went down to the Bank and bought that note. Just like an Englishman, you see; pluck to the backbone. Then he dictated a letter, which one of his clerks wrote out in a beautiful round hand, and the two brothers sat at the window a whole day watching for the right man to give it to.

They saw many honest faces go by that

were not intelligent enough; many that were intelligent, but not honest enough; many that were both, but the possessors were not poor enough, or, if poor enough, were not strangers. There was always a defect, until I came along; but they agreed that I filled the bill all around, so they elected me unanimously; and there I was now, waiting to know why I was called in. They began to ask me questions about myself, and pretty soon they had my story. Finally, they told me I would answer their purpose. I said I was sincerely glad, and asked what it was. Then one of them handed me an envelope, and said I would find the explanation inside. I was going to open it, but he said no, take it to my lodgings and look it over carefully, and not be hasty or rash. I was puzzled, and wanted to discuss the matter a little further, but they didn't; so I took my leave, feeling hurt and insulted to be made the butt of what was apparently some kind of a practical joke, and yet obliged to put up with it, not being in circumstances to resent affronts from rich and strong folk.

I would have picked up the pear now and

eaten it before all the world, but it was gone; so I had lost that by this unlucky business, and the thought of it did not soften my feeling towards those men. As soon as I was out of sight of that house I opened my envelope, and saw that it contained money! My opinion of those people changed, I can tell you! I lost not a moment, but shoved note and money into my vest pocket, and broke for the nearest cheap eating house. Well, how I did eat! When at last I couldn't hold any more, I took out my money and unfolded it, took one glimpse and nearly fainted. Five millions of dollars! Why, it made my head swim.

I must have sat there, stunned and blinking at the note, as much as a minute before I came rightly to myself again. The first thing I noticed, then, was the landlord. His eye was on the note, and he was petrified. He was worshiping, with all his body and soul, but he looked as if he couldn't stir hand or foot. I took my cue in a moment, and did the only rational thing there was to do. I reached the note towards him, and said, carelessly:

"Give me the change, please."

Then he was restored to his normal condition, and made a thousand apologies for not being able to break the bill, and I couldn't get him to touch it. He wanted to look at it, and keep on looking at it; he couldn't seem to get enough of it to quench the thirst of his eye, but he shrank from touching it as if it had been something too sacred for poor common clay to handle. I said: "I am sorry if it is an inconvenience, but I must insist. Please change it; I haven't anything else."

But he said that wasn't any matter; he was quite willing to let the trifle stand over till another time. I said I might not be in his neighbourhood again for a good while; but he said it was of no consequence, he could wait, and, moreover, I could have anything I wanted, any time I chose, and let the account run as long as I pleased. He said he hoped he wasn't afraid to trust as rich a gentleman as I was, merely because I was of a merry disposition, and chose to play larks on the public in the matter of dress. By this time another customer was entering, and the landlord hinted to me to put the monster out of sight; then he bowed me all the way to the door. I started straight for that house and those brothers, to correct the mistake which had been made before the police should hunt me up, and help me do it. I was pretty nervous; in fact, pretty badly frightened, though of course, I was no way in fault. But I knew men well enough to know that when they find they've given a tramp a million-pound bill when they thought it was a one-pounder, they are in a frantic rage against him instead of quarrelling with their own nearsightedness, as they ought. As I approached the house, my excitement began to abate – for all was quiet there, which made me feel pretty sure the blunder was not discovered yet. I rang. The same servant appeared. I asked for those gentlemen.

"They are gone." This in the lofty, cold way of that fellow's tribe.

"Gone? Gone where?"

"On a journey."

"But whereabouts?"

"To the Continent, I think."

"The Continent?"

"Yes, sir."

"Which way – by what route?"

"I can't say, sir."

"When will they be back?"

"In a month, they said."

"A month! Oh, this is awful! Give me some sort of idea of how to get a word to them. It's of the utmost importance."

"I can't, indeed. I've no idea where they've gone, sir."

"Then I must see some member of the family."

"Family's away, too; been abroad months – in Egypt and India, I think."

"Man, there's been an immense mistake made. They'll be back before night. Will you tell them I've been here, and that I will keep coming till it's all made right, and they needn't be afraid?"

"I'll tell them, if they come back, but I am not expecting them. They said you would be here in an hour to make enquiries, but I must tell you it's all right, they'll be here on time and expect you."

So I had to give it up and go away. What a riddle it all was! I was like to lose my mind. They would be here "on time". What could that mean? Oh, the letter would explain, maybe. I had forgotten the letter; I got it out and read it. This is what it said:

> *You are an intelligent and honest man, as one may see by your face. We conceive you to be poor and a stranger. Enclosed you will find a sum of money. It is lent to you for thirty days, without interest. Report at this house at the end of that time. I have a bet on you. If I win it, you shall have any situation that is in my gift – any, that is, that you shall be able to prove yourself familiar with and competent to fill.*

No signature, no address, no date.

Well, here was a coil to be in! You are posted on what had preceded all this, but I was not. It was just a deep, dark puzzle to me. I hadn't the least idea what the game was, nor whether harm was meant me, or a kindness. I went into a park and sat down to try to think it out, and to consider what I had best do.

At the end of an hour my reasonings had crystallised into this verdict.

Maybe those men mean me well, maybe they mean me ill; no way to decide that – let it go. They've got a game, or a scheme, or an experiment of some kind on hand; no way to determine what it is. Let it go. There's a bet on me; no way to find out what it is. Let it go.

That disposes of the indeterminable quantities; the remainder of the matter is tangible, solid, and may be classed and labelled with certainty. If I ask the Bank of England to place this bill to the credit of the man it belongs to, they'll do it, for they know him, although I don't; but they will ask me how I came into possession of it, and if I tell the truth, they'll put me in the asylum, naturally; a lie will land me in jail. The same result would follow if I tried to bank the bill anywhere, or to borrow money on it. I have got to carry this immense burden around until those men come back, whether I want to or not. It is useless to me, as useless as a handful of ashes, and yet I must take care of it, and watch over it, while I beg my living. I couldn't give it away if I should try, for neither honest citizen nor highwayman would accept it or meddle with it for anything. Those brothers are safe. Even if I lose their bill, or burn it, they are still safe, because they can stop payment, and the Bank will make them whole; but meantime I've got to do a month's suffering without wages or profit - unless I help win that bet, whatever it may be, and get that situation that I am promised. I should like to get that; men of their sort have situations in their gift that are worth having.

I got to thinking a good deal about that situation. My hopes began to rise high. Without doubt, the salary would be large. It would begin in a month; after that, I should be all right. Pretty soon I was feeling first-rate. By this time, I was tramping the streets again. The sight of a tailor shop gave me a sharp longing to shed my rags, and to clothe myself decently once more. Could I afford it?

No; I had nothing in the world but a million pounds. So I forced myself to go on by. But soon I was drifting back again. The temptation persecuted me cruelly. I must have passed that shop back and forth six times during that manful struggle. At last I gave in; I had to. I asked if they had a misfit suit that had been thrown on their hands. The fellow I spoke to nodded his head towards another fellow, and gave me no answer. I went to the indicated fellow, and he indicated another fellow with his head, and no words. I went to *him*, and he said: "Tend to you presently."

I waited till he was done with what he was at; then he took me into a back room, overhauled a pile of rejected suits and selected the rattiest one for me. I put it on. It didn't fit, and wasn't in any way attractive, but it was new, and I was anxious to have it; so I didn't find any fault, but said, with some diffidence: "It would be an accommodation to me if you could wait some days for the money. I haven't any small change about me."

The fellow worked up a most sarcastic

expression of countenance, and said: "Oh, you haven't? Well, of course, I didn't expect it. I'd only expect gentlemen like you to carry large change."

I was nettled, and said: "My friend, you shouldn't judge a stranger always by the clothes he wears. I am quite able to pay for this suit; I simply didn't wish to put you to the trouble of changing a large note."

He modified his style a little at that, and said, though still with something of an air: "I didn't mean any particular harm, but as long as rebukes are going, I might say it wasn't quite your affair to jump to the conclusion that we couldn't change any note that you might happen to be carrying around. On the contrary, we can."

I handed the note to him, and said: "Oh, very well; I apologise."

He received it with a smile, one of those large smiles that goes all around over, and has folds in it, and wrinkles, and spirals, and looks like the place where you have thrown a brick in a pond; and then in the act of taking a glimpse of the bill, this smile froze solid and turned yellow, and looked like those wavy, wormy spreads of lava that you find hardened on little levels on the side of Vesuvius. I never before saw a smile caught like that, and perpetuated. The man stood there holding the bill, looking like that, and the proprietor hustled up to see what was the matter and said, briskly:

"Well, what's up? What's the trouble? What's wanting?"

I said: "There isn't any trouble. I'm waiting for my change."

"Come, come, get him his change, Tod; get him his change."

Tod retorted: "Get him his change! It's easy to say, sir; but look at the bill yourself."

The proprietor took a look, gave a low, eloquent whistle, then made a dive for the pile of rejected clothing and began to snatch it this way and that, talking all the time excitedly, and as if to himself:

"Sell an eccentric millionaire such an unspeakable suit as that! Tod's a fool – a born fool. Always doing

something like this. Drives every millionaire away from this place, because he can't tell a millionaire from a tramp, and never could ... Ah, here's the thing I am after. Please get those things off, sir, and throw them in the fire. Do me the favour to put on this shirt and this suit; it's just the thing, the very thing - plain, rich, modest and just ducally nobby, made to order for a foreign prince. You may know him, sir, his Serene Highness the Hospodar of Halifax; had to leave it with us and take a mourning-suit, because his mother was going to die - which she didn't. But that's all right; we can't always have things the way we - that is, the way they ... there! Trousers all right, they fit you to a charm, sir; now the waistcoat; aha, right again! Now the coat - Lord! Look at that, now! Perfect, the whole thing! I never saw such a triumph in all my experience."

I expressed my satisfaction.

"Quite right, sir, quite right; it'll do for a makeshift, I'm bound to say. But wait till you see what we'll get up for you on your own measure. Come, Tod, book and pen; get at it.

Length of leg, 32" - and so on. Before I could get in a word, he had measured me and was giving orders for dress suits, morning suits, shirts and all sorts of things. When I got a chance, I said:

"But, my dear sir, I can't give these orders, unless you can wait indefinitely, or change the bill."

"Indefinitely! It's a weak word, sir, a weak word. *Eternally* - that's the word, sir. Tod, rush these things through and send them to the gentleman's address without any waste of time. Let the minor customers wait. Set down the gentleman's address and -"

"I'm changing my quarters. I will drop in and leave the new address."

"Quite right, sir, quite right. One moment ... let me show you out, sir. There ... good day, sir, good day."

Well, don't you see what was bound to happen? I drifted naturally into buying whatever I wanted, and asking for change. Within a week, I was sumptuously equipped with all needful comforts and luxuries, and was housed in an expensive private hotel in Hanover Square. I took my dinners there, but for breakfast I stuck by Harris's humble feeding house, where I had got my first meal on my million-pound bill. I was the making of Harris. The fact had gone all abroad that the foreign crank who carried million-pound bills in his vest pocket was the patron saint of the place. That was enough. From being a poor, struggling, little hand-to-mouth enterprise, it had become celebrated and overcrowded with customers. Harris was so grateful that he forced loans upon me, and would not be denied; and so, pauper as I was, I had money to spend and was living like the rich and the great.

I judged that there was going to be a crash by and by, but I was in now and must swim across or drown. You see, there was just that element of impending disaster to give a serious side, a sober side, yes, a tragic side, to a state of things that would otherwise have been purely ridiculous. In the night, in the dark, the tragedy part was always to the front, and always warning, always threatening; and so I moaned and tossed, and sleep was hard to find. But in the cheerful daylight, the tragedy element faded out and disappeared, and I walked on air, and was happy to giddiness, to intoxication, you may say.

And it was natural; for I had become one of the notorieties of this metropolis of the world, and it turned my head, not just a little, but a good deal. You could not take up a newspaper, English, Scottish or Irish, without finding in it one or more references to the "vest-pocket million-pounder" and his latest doings and sayings. At first, in these mentions, I was at the bottom of the personal-gossip column; next, I was listed above the knights, next above the baronets, next above the barons and so on, climbing steadily as my notoriety augmented, until I reached the highest altitude possible – and there I remained, taking precedence among all dukes not royal, and of all ecclesiastics except the primate of all England.

But mind, this was not fame; as yet, I had achieved only notoriety. Then came the climaxing stroke – the accolade, so to speak – which, in a single instant, transmuted the perishable dross of notoriety into the enduring gold of fame: *Punch* caricatured me! Yes, I was a made man now; my place was established. I might be joked about still, but reverently, not hilariously, not rudely; I could be smiled at, but not laughed at. The time for that had gone by. *Punch* pictured me all a-flutter with rags, dickering with a beefeater for the Tower of London. Well, you can imagine how it was with a young fellow who had never been taken notice of before, and now all of a sudden couldn't say a thing that wasn't taken up and repeated everywhere; couldn't stir abroad without constantly overhearing the remark flying from lip to lip, *"There he goes; that's him!"* couldn't take his breakfast without a crowd to look on; couldn't appear in an opera box without concentrating there the fire of a thousand lorgnettes. Why, I just swam in glory all day long – that is the amount of it.

You know, I even kept my old suit of rags, and every now and then appeared in them, so as to have the old pleasure of buying trifles and being insulted, then shooting the scoffer dead with the million-pound bill. But I couldn't keep that up. The illustrated papers made the outfit so familiar that when I went out in it, I was at once recognised and followed by a crowd, and if I attempted a purchase the man would offer me his whole shop on credit before I could pull my note on him.

About the tenth day of my fame I went to fulfil my duty to my flag by paying my respects to the American minister. He received me with the enthusiasm proper in my case, upbraided me for being so tardy in my duty and said that there was only one way to get his forgiveness, and that was to take the seat at his dinner party that night made vacant by the illness of one of his guests. I said I would, and we got to talking. It turned out that he and my father had been schoolmates in boyhood, Yale students together later, and always warm friends up to my father's death. So then he required me to put in at his house all the odd time I might have to spare, and I was very willing, of course.

In fact, I was more than willing; I was glad. When the crash should come, he might somehow be able to save me from total destruction; I didn't know how, but he might think of a way, maybe. I couldn't venture to unbosom myself to him at this late date, a thing I would have been quick to do in the beginning of this awful career of mine in London. No, I couldn't venture it now. I was in too deep; that is, too deep for me to be risking revelations to so new a friend, though not clear beyond my depth, as I looked at it. Because, you see, with all my borrowing, I was carefully keeping within my means - I mean, within my salary. Of course, I couldn't know what my salary was going to be, but I had a good enough basis for an estimate in the fact that, if I won the bet, I was to have choice of any situation in that rich old gentleman's gift provided I was competent - and I should certainly prove competent. I hadn't any doubt about that. And as to the bet, I wasn't worrying about that; I had always been lucky.

Now, my estimate of the salary was six hundred to a thousand a year; say, six hundred for the first year and so on, up year by year, till

I struck the upper figure by proved merit. At present, I was only in debt for my first year's salary. Everybody had been trying to lend me money, but I had fought off most of them on one pretext or another, so this indebtedness represented only £300 borrowed money; the other £300 represented my keep and my purchases. I believed my second year's salary would carry me through the rest of the month if I went on being cautious and economical, and I intended to look sharply out for that. My month ended, my employer back from his journey, I should be all right once more, for I should at once divide the two years' salary among my creditors by assignment and get right down to my work.

It was a lovely dinner party of fourteen. The Duke and Duchess of Shoreditch, and their daughter the Lady Anne-Grace-Eleanor-Celeste-and-so-forth-and-so-forth-de-Bohun, the Earl and Countess of Newgate, Viscount Cheapside, Lord and Lady Blatherskite, some untitled people of both sexes, the minister and his wife and daughter, and his daughter's visiting friend, an English girl of twenty-two named Portia Langham, whom I fell in love with in two minutes, and she with me - I could see it without glasses. There was still another guest, an American - but I am a little ahead of my story. While the people were still in the drawing room, whetting up for dinner and coldly inspecting the latecomers, the servant announced: "Mr Lloyd Hastings."

The moment the usual civilities were over, Hastings caught sight of me and came straight with cordially outstretched hand, then stopped short when about to shake and said, with an embarrassed look: "I beg your pardon, sir, I thought I knew you."

"Why, you do know me, old fellow."

"No. Are you the - the-"

"Vest-pocket monster? I am, indeed. Don't be afraid to call me by my nickname; I'm used to it."

"Well, well, well, this is a surprise. Once or twice I've seen your own name coupled with the nickname, but it never occurred to me that you could be the 'Henry Adams' referred to. Why, it isn't six months since you were clerking away for Blake Hopkins in Frisco on a salary, and sitting up nights on an extra allowance, helping me arrange and verify the Gould and Curry Extension papers and statistics! The idea of your being in London, and a vast millionaire, and a colossal celebrity! Why, it's the *Arabian Nights* come again. Man, I can't take it in at all; can't realise it; give me time to settle the whirl in my head."

"The fact is, Lloyd, you are no worse off than I am. I can't realise it myself."

"Dear me, it is stunning, now, isn't it? Why, it's just three months today since we went to the Miners' restaurant -"

"No; the What Cheer."

"Right, it was the What Cheer; went there at two in the morning and had a chop and coffee after a hard six-hours grind over those Extension papers, and I tried to persuade you to come to London with me, and offered to get leave of absence for you and pay all your expenses, and give you something over if I succeeded in making the sale. And you would not listen to me, said I wouldn't succeed, and you couldn't afford to lose the run of business and be no end of time getting the hang of things again when you got back home. And yet here you are. How odd it all is! How did you happen to come, and whatever did give you this incredible start?"

"Oh, just an accident. It's a long story - a romance, a body may say. I'll tell you all about it, but not now."

"When?"

"The end of this month."

"That's more than a fortnight yet! It's too much of a strain on a person's curiosity. Make it a week."

"I can't. You'll know why, by and by. But how's the trade getting along?"

His cheerfulness vanished like a breath, and he said with a sigh: "You were a true prophet, Hal, a true prophet. I wish I hadn't come. I don't want to talk about it."

"But you must. You must come and stop with me tonight, when we leave here, and tell me all about it."

"Oh, may I? Are you in earnest?" And the water showed in his eyes.

"Yes; I want to hear the whole story, every word."

"I'm so grateful! Just to find a human interest once more, in some voice and in some eye, in me and affairs of mine, after what I've been through here – Lord! I could go down on my knees for it!"

He gripped my hand hard, and braced up, and was all right and lively after that for the dinner – which didn't come off. No, the usual thing happened, the thing that is always happening under that vicious and aggravating English system: the matter of precedence couldn't be settled, and so there was no dinner. Englishmen always eat dinner before they go out to dinner, because they know the risks they are running; but nobody ever warns the stranger, and so he walks placidly into trap. Of course, nobody was hurt this time, because we had all been to dinner, none of us being novices excepting Hastings, and he having been informed by the minister at the time that he invited him that, in deference to the English custom, he had not provided any dinner.

Everybody took a lady and processioned down to the dining room, because it is usual to go through the motions; but there the dispute began. The Duke of Shoreditch wanted to take precedence and sit at the head of the table, holding that he outranked a minister who represented merely a nation and not a monarch; but I stood for my rights, and refused to yield. In the gossip column, I ranked all dukes not royal, and said so, and claimed precedence of this one. It couldn't be settled, of course, struggle as we might and did, he finally (and injudiciously) trying to play birth and antiquity and I "seeing" his Conqueror and "raising" him with Adam, whose direct posterity I was, as shown by my name, while he was of a collateral branch, as shown by his, and by his recent Norman origin; so we all processioned back to the drawing room again and had a perpendicular lunch - plate of sardines and a strawberry, and you group yourself and stand up and eat it. Here the religion of precedence is not so strenuous; the two persons of highest rank chuck up a shilling, the one that wins has first go at his strawberry, and the loser gets the shilling. The next two chuck up, then the next two, and so on. After refreshment, tables were brought, and we all played cribbage, sixpence a game. The English never play any game for amusement. If they can't make something or lose something - they don't care which - they won't play.

We had a lovely time; certainly, two of us had, Miss Langham and I. I was so bewitched with her that I couldn't count my hands if they went above a double sequence; and when I struck home I never discovered it, and started up the outside row again, and would have lost the game every time, only the girl did the same, she being in just my condition, you see. Consequently, neither of us ever got out, or cared to wonder why we didn't; we only just knew we were happy, and didn't wish to know anything else, and didn't want to be interrupted. And I told her - I did, indeed - told her I loved her; and she - well, she blushed till her hair turned red, but she liked it; she said she did. Oh, there was never such an evening! Every time I pegged I put on a postscript; every time she pegged she acknowledged receipt of it, counting the hands the same. Why, I couldn't even say "two for his heels" without adding: "My, how sweet you do look!" And she would say: "Fifteen two, fifteen four, fifteen six and a pair are eight, and eight are sixteen - do you think so?" - peeping out aslant from under her lashes, you know, so sweet and cunning. Oh, it was just too-too!

Well, I was perfectly honest and square with her; told her I hadn't a cent in the world but just the million-pound note she'd heard so much talk about, and it didn't belong to me, and that started her curiosity; and then I talked low, and told her the whole history right from the start, and it nearly killed her laughing. What in the nation she could find to laugh about I couldn't see, but there it was; every half-minute some new detail would fetch her, and I would have to stop as much as a minute and a half to give her a chance to settle down again. Why, she laughed herself lame - she did, indeed. I never saw anything like it. I mean, I never saw a painful story - a story of a person's troubles and worries and fears - produce just that kind of effect before. So I loved her all the more, seeing she could be so cheerful when there wasn't anything to be cheerful about; for I might soon need that kind of wife, you know, the way things looked. Of course, I told her we should have to wait a couple of years, till I could catch up on my salary; but she didn't mind that, only she hoped I would be as careful as possible in the matter of expenses, and not let them run the least risk of trenching on our third year's pay. Then she began to get a little worried, and wondered if we were making any mistake and starting the salary on a higher figure for the first year than I would get. This was good sense, and it made me feel a little less confident than I had been feeling before; but it gave me a good business idea, and I brought it frankly out.

"Portia, dear, would you mind going with

me that day, when I confront those old gentlemen?"

She shrank a little, but said: "N-o; if my being with you would help hearten you. But - would it be quite proper, do you think?"

"No, I don't know that it would - in fact, I'm afraid it wouldn't; but, you see, there's so much dependent upon it that -"

"Then I'll go anyway, proper or improper," she said, with a beautiful and generous enthusiasm. "Oh, I shall be so happy to think I'm helping!"

"Helping, dear? Why, you'll be doing it all. You're so beautiful and so lovely and so winning, that with you there I can pile our salary up till I break those good old fellows, and they'll never have the heart to struggle."

Sho! You should have seen the rich blood mount, and her happy eyes shine!

"You wicked flatterer! There isn't a word of truth in what you say, but still I'll go with you. Maybe it will teach you not to expect other people to look with your eyes."

Were my doubts dissipated? Was my

confidence restored? You may judge by this fact: privately, I raised my salary to twelve hundred the first year on the spot. But I didn't tell her; I saved it for a surprise.

All the way home I was in the clouds, Hastings talking, I not hearing a word. When he and I entered my parlour, he brought me to myself with his fervent appreciations of my manifold comforts and luxuries.

"Let me just stand here a little and look my fill. Dear me! it's a palace - it's just a palace! And in it everything a body could desire, including cosy coal fire and supper standing ready. Henry, it doesn't merely make me realise how rich you are; it makes me realise, to the bone, to the marrow, how poor I am - how poor I am, and how miserable, how defeated, routed, annihilated!"

Plague take it! this language gave me the cold shudders. It scared me broad awake, and made me comprehend that I was standing on a half-inch crust, with a crater underneath. I didn't know I had been dreaming - that is, I hadn't been allowing myself to know it for a while back; but now - oh, dear! Deep in debt, not a cent in the world, a lovely girl's happiness or woe in my hands and nothing in front of me but a salary which might never - oh, *would* never - materialise! Oh, oh, oh! I am ruined past hope! nothing can save me!

"Henry, the mere unconsidered drippings of your daily income would -"

"Oh, my 'daily income'! Here, down with this hot scotch, and cheer up your soul. Here's with you! Or, no - you're hungry; sit down and -"

"Not a bite for me; I'm past it. I can't eat these days; but I'll drink with you till I drop. Come!"

"Barrel for barrel, I'm with you! Ready? Here we go! Now, then, Lloyd, unreel your story while I brew."

"Unreel it? What, again?"

"Again? What do you mean by that?"

"Why, I mean do you want to hear it over again?"

"Do I want to hear it over again? This is a puzzler. Wait; don't take any more of that liquid. You don't need it."

"Look here, Henry, you alarm me. Didn't I tell you the whole story on the way here?"

"You?"

"Yes, I."

"I'll be hanged if I heard a word of it."

"Henry, this is a serious thing. It troubles me. What did you take up yonder at the minister's?"

Then it all flashed on me, and I owned up like a man. "I took the dearest girl in this world ... prisoner!"

So then he came with a rush, and we shook, and shook, and shook till our hands ached; and he didn't blame me for not having heard a word of a story that had lasted while we walked three miles. He just sat down then, like the patient, good fellow he was, and told it all over again. Synopsised, it amounted to this: he had come to England with what he thought was a grand opportunity; he had an "option" to sell the Gould and Curry Extension for the "locators" of it, and keep all he could get over a million dollars. He had worked hard, had pulled every wire he knew of, had left no honest expedient untried, had spent nearly all the money he had in the world, had not been able to get a solitary capitalist to listen to him – and his option would run out at the end of the month. In a word, he was ruined.

Then he jumped up and cried out: "Henry, you can save me! You can save me, and you're the only man in the universe that can. Will you do it? Won't you do it?"

"Tell me how. Speak out, my boy."

"Give me a million and my passage home for my 'option'! Don't, don't refuse!"

I was in a kind of agony. I was right on the point of coming out with the words *Lloyd, I'm a pauper myself, absolutely penniless, and in debt!*

But a white-hot idea came flaming through my head, and I gripped my jaws together and calmed myself down till I was as cold as a capitalist. Then I said, in a commercial and self-possessed way:

"I will save you, Lloyd –"

"Then I'm already saved! God be merciful to you forever! If ever I –"

"Let me finish, Lloyd. I will save you, but not in that way; for that would not be fair to you, after your hard work and the risks you've run. I don't need to buy mines. I can keep my capital moving, in a commercial centre like London, without that; it's what I'm at, all the time. But here is what I'll do. I know all about that mine, of course; I know its immense value, and can swear to it if anybody wishes it. You shall sell out inside of the fortnight for three million cash, using my name freely, and we'll divide, share and share alike."

Do you know, he would have danced the furniture to kindling-wood in his insane joy, and broken everything in the place, if I hadn't tripped him up and tied him. Then he lay there, perfectly happy, saying: "I may use your name! Your name – think of it! Man, they'll flock in droves, these rich Londoners; they'll fight for that stock! I'm a made man, I'm a made man forever, and I'll never forget you as long as I live!"

In less than twenty-four hours London was abuzz! I hadn't anything to do, day after day, but sit at home, and say to all comers: "Yes; I told him to refer to me. I know the man, and I know the mine. His character is above reproach, and the mine is worth far more than he asks for it."

Meantime, I spent all my evenings at the minister's with Portia. I didn't say a word to her about the mine; I saved it for a surprise. We talked salary, never anything but salary and love; sometimes love, sometimes salary, sometimes love and salary together. And my! The interest the minister's wife and daughter took in our little affair, and the endless ingenuities they invented to save us from interruption, and to keep the minister in the dark and unsuspicious - well, it was just lovely of them!

When the month was up at last, I had a million dollars to my credit in the London and County Bank, and Hastings was fixed in the same way. Dressed my level best, I drove by the house in Portland Place, judged by the look of things that my birds were home again, went on towards the minister's and got my precious, and we started back, talking salary with all our might. She was so excited and anxious that it made her just intolerably beautiful. I said:

"Dearie, the way you're looking, it's a crime to strike for a salary a single penny under three thousand a year."

"Henry, Henry, you'll ruin us!"

"Don't you be afraid. Just keep up those looks, and trust to me. It'll all come out right."

So, as it turned out, I had to keep bolstering her courage all the way. She kept pleading with me, saying: "Oh, please remember that if we ask for too much, we may get no salary at all; and then what will become of us, with no way in the world to earn our living?"

We were ushered in by that same servant, and there they were, the two old gentlemen. Of course, they were surprised to see that wonderful creature with me, but I said: "It's all right, gentlemen; she is my future stay and helpmate."

And I introduced them to her, and called them by name. It didn't surprise them; they knew I would know enough to consult the directory. They seated us, and were very polite to me, and very solicitous to relieve her from embarrassment, and put her as much at her ease as they could. Then I said: "Gentlemen, I am ready to report."

"We are glad to hear it," said my man, "for now we can decide the bet which my brother Abel and I made. If you have won for me, you shall have any situation in my gift. Have you the million-pound note?"

"Here it is, sir," and I handed it to him.

"I've won!" he shouted, and slapped Abel on the back. "Now what do you say, brother?"

"I say he did survive, and I've lost twenty thousand pounds. I never would have believed it."

"I've a further report to make," I said, "and a pretty long one. I want you to let me come soon, and detail my whole month's history; and I promise you it's worth hearing. Meantime, take a look at that."

"What, man! Certificate of deposit for £200,000. Is it yours?"

"Mine. I earned it by thirty days' judicious use of that little loan you let me have. And the only use I made of it was to buy trifles and offer the bill in change."

"Come, this is astonishing! It's incredible, man!"

"Never mind, I'll prove it. Don't take my word unsupported."

But now Portia's turn was come to be surprised. Her eyes were spread wide, and she said: "Henry, is that really your money? Have you been fibbing to me?"

"I have, indeed, dearie. But you'll forgive me, I know."

She put up an arch pout, and said: "Don't you be so sure. You are a naughty thing to deceive me so!"

"Oh, you'll get over it, sweetheart, you'll get over it; it was only fun, you know. Come, let's be going."

"But wait, wait! The situation, you know. I want to give you the situation," said my man.

"Well," I said, "I'm just as grateful as I can be, but really, I don't want one."

"But you can have the very choicest one in my gift."

"Thanks again, with all my heart; but I don't even want that one."

"Henry, I'm ashamed of you. You don't half thank the good gentleman. May I do it for you?"

"Indeed, you shall, dear, if you can improve it. Let us see you try."

She walked to my man, got up in his lap, put her arm round his neck, and kissed him right on the mouth. Then the two old gentlemen shouted with laughter, but I was dumfounded, just petrified, as you may say. Portia said: "Papa, he has said you haven't a situation in your gift that he'd take; and I feel just as hurt as –"

"My darling, is that your *papa*?"

"Yes; he's my step-papa, and the dearest one that ever was. You understand now, don't you, why I was able to laugh when you told me at the minister's, not knowing my relationships, what trouble and worry Papa's and Uncle Abel's scheme was giving you?"

Of course, I spoke right up now, without any fooling, and went straight to the point: "Oh, my dearest dear sir, I want to take back what I said. You have got a situation open that I want."

"Name it."

"Son-in-law."

"Well, well, well! But you know, if you haven't ever served in that capacity, you, of course, can't furnish recommendations of a sort to satisfy the conditions of the contract, and so -"

"Try me - oh, do, I beg of you! Only just try me thirty or forty years, and if -"

"Oh, well, all right; it's but a little thing to ask; take her along."

Happy, we two? There are not words enough in the *Unabridged* to describe it. And when London got the whole history, a day or two later, of my month's adventures with that banknote, and how they ended, did London talk, and have a good time? Yes.

My Portia's papa took that friendly and hospitable bill back to the Bank of England and cashed it; then the Bank cancelled it and made him a present of it, and he gave it to us at our wedding, and it has always hung in its frame in the sacredest place in our home ever since. For it gave me my Portia. But for it, I could not have remained in London, would not have appeared at the minister's, never should have met her. And so I always say: "Yes, it's a million-pounder, as you see; but it never made but one purchase in its life, and then got the article for only about a tenth part of its value."

Luck

Note: This is not a fancy sketch. I got it from a clergyman who was an instructor at Woolwich forty years ago, and who vouched for its truth. –MT

It was at a banquet in London in honour of one of the two or three conspicuously illustrious English military names of this generation. For reasons that will presently appear, I shall withhold his real name and titles and call him Lieutenant-General Lord Arthur Scoresby, VC, KCB, etc., etc., etc. What a fascination there is in a renowned name! There sat the man, in actual flesh, whom I had heard of so many thousands of times since that day, thirty years before, when his name shot suddenly to the zenith from a Crimean battlefield to remain forever celebrated. It was food and drink to me to look, and look, and look at that demigod, scanning, searching, noting: the quietness, the reserve, the noble gravity of his countenance; the simple honesty that expressed itself all over him; the sweet unconsciousness of his greatness - unconsciousness of the hundreds of admiring eyes fastened upon him, unconsciousness of the deep, loving, sincere worship welling out of the breasts of those people and flowing toward him.

The clergyman at my left was an old acquaintance of mine - clergyman now, but had spent the first half of his life in the camp and field, and as an instructor in the military school at Woolwich. Just at the moment I have been talking about, a veiled and singular light glimmered in his eyes, and he leaned down and muttered confidentially to me, indicating the hero of the banquet with a gesture: "Privately - his glory is an accident. Just a product of incredible luck."

This verdict was a great surprise to me. If

its subject had been Napoleon or Socrates or Solomon, my astonishment could not have been greater.

Some days later came the explanation of this strange remark, and this is what the Reverend told me:

"About forty years ago, I was an instructor in the military academy at Woolwich. I was present in one of the sections when young Scoresby underwent his preliminary examination. I was touched to the quick with pity; for the rest of the class answered up brightly and handsomely, while he - why, dear me, he didn't know anything, so to speak. He was evidently good, and sweet, and lovable, and guileless; and so it was exceedingly painful to see him stand there, as serene as a graven image, and deliver himself of answers which were veritably miraculous for stupidity and ignorance. All the compassion in me was aroused in his behalf. I said to myself, *when he comes to be examined again, he will be flung over, of course; so it will be simple a harmless act of charity to ease his fall as much as I can.*

"I took him aside, and found that he knew a little of Caesar's history; and as he didn't know anything else, I went to work and drilled him like a galley-slave on a certain line of stock questions concerning Caesar, which I knew would be used. If you'll believe me, he went through with flying colours on examination day! He went through on that purely superficial 'cram', and got compliments, too, while others, who knew a thousand times more than he, got plucked. By some strangely lucky accident – an accident not likely to happen twice in a century – he was asked no question outside of the narrow limits of his drill.

"It was stupefying. Well, although through his course I stood by him, with something of the sentiment that a mother feels for a crippled child; and he always saved himself – just by miracle, apparently.

"Now, of course, the thing that would expose him and kill him at last was mathematics. I resolved to make his death as easy as I could; so I drilled him and crammed him, and crammed him and drilled him, just on the line of questions the examiner would be most likely to use, and then launched him on his fate. Well, sir, try to conceive of the result: to my consternation, he took the first prize! And with it, he got a perfect ovation in the way of compliments.

"Sleep! There was no more sleep for me for a week. My conscience tortured me day and night. What I had done, I had done purely through charity, and only to ease the poor youth's fall – I never had dreamed of any such preposterous result as the thing that had happened. I felt as guilty and miserable as the creator of Frankenstein. Here was a woodenhead whom I had put in the way of glittering promotions and prodigious responsibilities, and but one thing could happen: he and his responsibilities would all go to ruin together at the first opportunity.

"The Crimean War had just broken out. *Of course, there had to be a war,* I said to myself, *we couldn't have peace and give this donkey a chance to die before he is found out.* I waited for the earthquake. It came. And it made me reel when it did come. He was actually gazetted to a captaincy in a marching regiment! Better men grow old and grey in the service before they climb to a sublimity like that. And who could ever have foreseen that they would go and put such a load of responsibility on such green and inadequate shoulders? I could just barely have stood it if they had made him a cornet; but a captain - think of it! I thought my hair would turn white.

"Consider what I did - I, who so loved repose and inaction. I said to myself, *I am responsible to the country for this, and I must go along with him and protect the country against him as far as I can.* So I took my poor little capital that I had saved up through years of work and grinding economy, and went with a sigh and bought a cornetcy in his regiment; and away we went to the field.

"And there - oh dear, it was awful. Blunders? Why, he never did anything *but* blunder. But, you see, nobody was in on the fellow's secret - everybody had him focused wrong, and necessarily misinterpreted his performance every time. Consequently, they took his idiotic blunders for inspirations of genius; they did, honestly! His mildest blunders were enough to make a man in his right mind cry; and they did make me cry, and rage and rave too, privately. And the thing that kept me always in a sweat of apprehension was the fact that every fresh blunder he made increased the lustre of his reputation! I kept saying to myself, *he'll get so high that when discovery does finally come, it will be like the sun falling out of the sky.*

"He went right along up, from grade to grade, over the dead bodies of his superiors, until at last, in the hottest moment of the battle of ———, down went our colonel, and my heart jumped into my mouth, for Scoresby was next in rank! *Now for it,* said I; *we'll all land in Sheol in ten minutes, sure.*

"The battle was awfully hot; the allies were steadily giving way all over the field. Our regiment occupied a position that was vital; a blunder now must be destruction. At this critical moment, what does this immortal fool do but detach the regiment from its place and order a charge over a neighbouring hill, where there wasn't a suggestion of an enemy! *There you go!* I said to myself, *this is the end at last.*

"And away we did go, and were over the shoulder of the hill before the insane movement could be discovered and stopped. And what did we find? An entire and unsuspected Russian army in reserve! And what happened? We were eaten up? That is necessarily what *would* have happened in ninety-nine cases out of a hundred.

"But no; those Russians argued that no single regiment would come browsing around there at such a time. It must be the entire English army, and that the sly Russian game was detected and blocked; so they turned tail, and away they went, pell-mell, over the hill and down into the field, in wild confusion, and we after them; they themselves broke the solid Russia centre in the field and tore through, and in no time there was the most tremendous rout you ever saw, and the defeat of the allies was turned into a sweeping and splendid victory! Marshal Canrobert looked on, dizzy with astonishment, admiration and delight, and sent right off for Scoresby, and hugged him, and decorated him on the field in presence of all the armies!

"And what was Scoresby's blunder that time? Merely the mistaking his right hand for his left - that was all. An order had come to him to fall back and support our right; and instead, he fell forward and went over the hill to the left. But the name he won that day as a marvellous military genius filled the world with his glory, and that glory will never fade while history books last.

"He is just as good and sweet and lovable and unpretending as a man can be, but he doesn't know enough to come in when it rains. He has been pursued, day by day and year by year, by a most phenomenal and astonishing *luckiness*.

"He has been a shining soldier in all our wars for half a generation; he has littered his military life with blunders, and yet has never committed one that didn't make him a knight or a baronet or a lord or something. Look at his breast; why, he is just clothed in domestic and foreign decorations. Well, sir, every one of them is a record of some shouting stupidity or other; and, taken together, they are proof that the very best thing in all this world that can befall a man is to be born ... *lucky*."

NEW TITLES FROM PAPER + INK

Oscar Wilde
The Happy Prince & Other Stories

O. Henry
The Gift of the Magi & Other Stories

Guy de Maupassant
The Necklace & Other Stories

Katherine Mansfield
The Garden Party & Other Stories

D. H. Lawrence
The Rocking Horse Winner & Other Stories

Visit **www.paperand.ink** to subscribe and receive the other books by post, as well as to keep up to date about new volumes in the series.